one cup: of poems.
Copyright (c) 2024 Hakeela Buford

For information:
AF.FORD MEDIA, LLC
15826 S LaGrange Road, Ste. 265
Orland Park, IL 60462

AF.FORD
BOOKS
An Imprint Division of AF.FORD MEDIA, LLC

Printed in the United States of America

979-8-9880203-6-3 (print) 979-8-9880203-7-0 (ebook)

Cover design, illustrations, and interior design by
AF.FORD MEDIA, LLC

one cup

OF POEMS

Hakeela Buford

To every person out there,
Including the ones who don't say much,
Who need every word to count:

Let each page that soon follows
Be a drop
Until you are full
(With no question)

Cup of contents
Where to fill that cup:

Cup of contents
Where to fill that cup:

Preface

We're all one

vessel.

So we're all
filling up

one another's cup.

One page

At a time.

Preface

We're all one

vessel.

So we're all
filling up

one another's cup.

One page

At a time.

The Places Where We Land Soft

...Hopefully
& Other Intimate Spaces

I woke up
to a sinkhole in my backyard.

That's right.

Before I turned off the lights,

There was a sink
In my home
And now, there's a sink
Hole in my backyard.

And what do you know

Last night,
It swallowed me up
While I was asleep.

But isn't that what they're supposed to be?
Sinks
With holes?
Putting it all underneath?

You're probably wondering how
I'm telling this story right now,

Awoke
And still living right now
And saying I survived.

But isn't that what you did last night,
Every night
When you go to sleep?

ONE CUP

KEELA BUFORD

Cupped

Like the cheeks
of
your face
In the hands
of
the one who now holds them

And hoping they don't release
You back
Into the land
You were just scooped up from

But also
That they don't make you
Over time
Reconsider

In their hands

How to romance an artist out of their paintbrushes, out of their studios

Compliment us

There's no better turn on
No other way

Compliment us

Not on our looks
But
On the looks
of what we create

Our art is the way
to our heart

No better turn on
No other way

Especially if
with these hands with which we've painted, molded, crafted
We're finally brave enough to take this cup of ours
And share it with you

And rather than to be quick to drink from it,
You say,
I love it, what you create,
what you do.

All Dawgz Go To Heaven (After the World Cup)

See em one minute
Called animals right from birth.
Sometimes (the) females, too
Oftentimes, the dog type
Right from jump.
And so, since the shoe must fit,
They sprint, run
That
Play
Too much
Sometimes for their own home court
advantage
Oftentimes, for someone else's joy

Sometimes
In the doghouse

After
Eliminating
The last drop
Out of places they've been
Prohibited to feast in
Because well,
The world is their cup

Getting licks
All the way to the buttom of the plates
No scrapes, *Only* wins
When there's so little provided
And still so much trying to be gained

See em next
Time up in the skies telling you
To
Cover all those bases,
Shoot all of those shots
Before someone else does

And get all of the fill,
All
That is rightfully yours

Make all of those goals,
Shoot all of those shots
Before someone else does

And damn sure all of the fill,
All that and more

Before
You join them

ONE CUP

Soft life

It's
crowding the hard corners
Broken appliances
Shattered cups and bowls

With pillows

Just filled with pillows

Soft life

It's
crowding the hard corners
Broken appliances
Shattered cups and bowls

Stores

always shopping around for stuff to make us…

Target and Walmart are dangerous.

I'm *only* coming in here for pillow–
No. Sock–

It-to-me cake–
Wait, nine dollars *off* porcelain plates??!

I guess…

And why not
It's a set, so some of these cups, too.

Now what do we do?
With a cart now full of cups,
Nothing but cups.
Far too expensive,
Even if they're on discount.

Even if they are porcelain.

Now look at you,
All of us,
Leaving out with
More than we came in
with, Much more
Than we bargained for.

A cart full of cups
And wondering how you're going to fill them,
How you're not going to *break*
Them

Which could've been avoided

Had you

Not forgotten the real thing
You came in for.

ONE CUP

Always shopping around for something to make us…

Get that speed fast
er Get into those size 7s quick
er Get that set of 100s easi
er Get that load whit
er Get those teeth whit

er…

Fit
ter
Small
er
Big
ger
Clean
er
Happi
er

Whole

Foods

laundry list

lots of stuff

to work on,
clean out,
if so

If we don't already know
how much stuff we already
store and hold.

Something weird's happening in aisle 7...

She just took it off the shelf and shoved it down
Her purse, mouth
Every single thing
In her eye level, her view,
In her grasp–

A few of the guys, too.
Right into
Their pockets–and then some.

Wait…
All of them
Are

Even though none
Of them are
On sale,

All full
Price.

Because at this point
Nothing's getting cheaper
But the quality anyways.

Because at this point
They care more about
Their bellies
Than their pockets

Staying full
Because nothing fully stays.

And even though none of them
Are on sale

They *are* all full
Price.

Finally, so thirsty, hungry to reclaim
Their value that was once their human right
And that they let someone else take in broad daylight
Now that's changed

On this night.
On this full moon.

KEELA BUFORD

Half Off

What we have
In our store.

That's on everything
Except

over there.

That stays full

Over there
In that aisle.

Why?

It's the one where we store
Our cups

And those are never half.

They're
Always
Full.

If we have anything to say about it.

And luckily,
We do

In our store.

Gyms

create gems

ONE CUP

They say ½ cup of milk, one scoop of protein makes you

Strong.   25

Made of 60% liquid
More or less, And the rest is
Protein.

Wouldn't it be nice if
We didn't have to work for it, came as-is?

Wouldn't it be nice if
That was the truth?

What if

It is?

Gyms Create Gems

That's why we go

Or why we avoid them.

Because we know

With just a bit of consistency, patience,
And sweat,
A drop at a time,

We'll find it already lying in our belly
Rock hard underneath:
Gym mines

For gems.

Just have to get a little wet.

Water Weight
(n)

1) When you think you weigh more
Than
You

Really do

But it's actually just
The old you

That you continue to
Sip

Here and there
Mixed with a lil
Salt

In attempt
To heal

Until

2) You finally realize
What's really been weighing you down the whole time
Is

The salt.

Overextended

My reach

Trying to grab
And pull down
All of the weight
Of all that collecting there

Like that base of sand anchoring down the punching bag
Like that water we run up against to test our hearts
Are still there and haven't washed away like the stamina
Of our legs

Like the weight
Of a body
Over its limit

That we keep trying
To push
When we need to be trying
To rest

A bit
More.

Overextended
My cup
And then,
Had to fill it up with Epsom salt

Because now,

I'm sore.

Rest Days

The one I dread
More than gym days
or
More than Mondays because I feel like,
Much like needed caught-up sleep or plans,
I'm being stopped while I'm
Almost ahead

Why don't we honor rest days?

To allow ourselves to recover
Instead of immediately going back to testing our
Limits
Our will
One day on top of another

We'd see we're limitless
Full
Of will
Power

That we purposely wilt
Water down

Because we fear what's starting to expand
And grow right before our eyes

And it's more than
We ever realized
Could materialize

But could also just as soon erase
As it did came

If we don't
Rise
To the occasion the very next day
And get back to striving
To maintain
This transformation we've strived so long for
And never thought we'd see

Like peace
After a storm

That could very possibly soon
Return once again

School & Work

How to know you (have a talent)

When you stop looking in yourself
For the clue
And start looking at everyone else
Around you
And the cups they're still drinking from
With your instruction
To handle with care

And they did
Because it was a gift

And only then
You realize
Has always been
A gift

Expectations

How do we expect people
To give to us
What they don't even give to themselves?

39

How do we expect

People
To fill up in us
What they don't even fill within themselves

Because they don't even have it to begin with?

Misplacing Cups That Don't Belong (to You)

By the time I got to high school
People didn't know where to place me

Good.

Because
People often want to place you
Only so that they can put you
In your place

By the time I got to high school
People didn't know where to place me
Which is good

Because
My cup isn't for placing
On your shelves or desks to hold your fill
Or anywhere else you feel
It belongs

My cup is not
Your cup

My cup is
Mine

And I'll place it
Only where I see fit
Even if that means it
Will try different
Places until it
Fills out what belongs
(In it and around it)

And so, that means it fits
Just fine

What if I told you that you are a…

Body of one
Made of glass
Or porcelain
Or sometimes ceramic

Or sometimes paper
like those small ones you fill with mouthwash,
only tolerable in small doses
Wanting to take it so easy

That you easily bend
Or break whenever something too sharp
Or weight
ed Or even harder
Than you
Comes weighing down on you
Into you
Right on through

You

What if I told you
that you only had one
body

That you have to handle with care,
no matter the outer packaging
you come here in,
especially when,
once
you have to entrust
yourself in many hands
or even just
the hands of
one
's
own

But what I can't tell you
is if you
are half empty
or
half full

That can only be told by one
And that one
Is
You and only you alone

KEELA BUFORD

I'm afraid to say I left
my cup at the office.

I left
it there
Right before
I left

And so, now it might be dusty

It might be
Filled up with something else

Other than my favorite daily remedy
I had to gulp down
To gulp down
The rest of the day that was shoved at me

Or it might be
Poured out for something else

They want to fill my cup
With

It might be a cup
I no longer need
Want
Like
The taste of

Or it might be because
They'll tell me to come back
Into the office

For my cup

That
I rushed and left
When I rushed and left
The office
They want me to report back to

And I no longer want to
Because
I'm now home
And now I know it's

Best,

PARTIES

...and Other Spaces Where We're Supposed to Be Happy

KEELA BUFORD

That one at the party/Teetotaler

It was handed over,
That cup

From their hand to yours.
And with one hand
You took it

Not realizing until after all this time
That
You already had a cup

In your other hand
That you brought with you
Always carry with you.

And then,
You have to look down at that hand,
That other hand
because you can't remember and need to see

did you leave it
back there.

Momma says once you put your drink down…

"You better leave it right there.
Don't pick it up again."

Someone I know in the family did
And she hasn't been
The same since.

See,
Once you consume some things
That have been sitting away from your sight
When you come back to it
Even though you can't taste it
Even though you don't know something's not quite right

Soon your body does

Because your body keeps the score.

And sometimes,
You're the one to lose

You

After consuming something no longer good
'Cause like momma says
Once you put your drink down
It's for your greater good

That you leave it there
'Cause you might not be okay
Like before,
Like you thought you were all those times
Before
When you used to

Leave it,
Leave it right there
And not pick it back up again
After you put it down.

After the party

There are so many broken dishes
So many crushed cups.

Who will be the one
To help pick each broken piece
Up?

That's always the big question
After the party.

Just like this one:
What do we do with the Solo ones,
Those red branded ones
So often released

Into the trash?

One Cup

And in it,

I wish you could get those infinite refills

Like you'd get at a buffet,

Kinda like Icees or that tub of cotton candy

Like you'd sometimes be allowed to

Get as a kid at the gas station or the movies.

Except this is real life

Playing right in front of our very eyes,

All we can eat

Until it's done.

AutoFill

Technology has a way of looking out for us
Don't even have to type out anything
Not even our next desires

Almost like
Love bombing
It feels sometimes

The way it's always looking out

Putting more and more constantly on our plates
Once it sees our feed growing empty

Almost like
If you squint, you see a glint
Around the feeders' heads, it feels sometimes

Of what appears to be
Not a halo but possibly
a sun rising just over them as they turn their heads one way
For us to better see the shimmer of their hair,
Or that 2000 square foot farm of theirs

Or their Ferrari
Odd flex, advertising for a barn

And we tap or swipe anyway, another which way
And out of it comes
More words
And more presentations
Through the screen
More and more words and presentations
Until we
Can't even get out

And in our pens,
Do we want to?
When there is the halo
Right in front of our eyes,
And the feed filling in
Right at our fingertips
Telling us it's not that bad
Being overfed?

Because who knows if we really can break free anymore,

Being overfed...
Besides, the feeling of feeling hunger again is much too
Much on all of our plates

Social Media Challenge

I'm serious
I'm going to do it

Make a post and it is just going to show
Nothing but
Cups.

Simply cups.

I might add different kinds
I might show some with rims
Some with handles
Some that are independent of one,
don't need the helping hand
or

that have snatched those hands off,
their jagged dips and rippled ridges to prove it.

I might even have some with tons of colors
Some just simply white
And some that just want to simply exist

As a cup.

But all of them my pottery
That I made.

I might
Get likes
I might get follows
I might get comments

Or I might
Get none of that,
Not understood.

But either way, it's all good.

Because at least
I'll have
My cups.

Still Outside

Churches, Beauty Shops, Saltwater Beaches, Bowling Alleys, Bars
&
Other Steadfast Third Places

Something we never think about, think is fascinating

Cups

Can be found in various places:

In our interlocked hands holding promises and surrender in our pews and temples
Under our outerwear to protect our most coveted parts
Right at our fingertips…but coming at a price

Passing by
Them all in the aisles.

Much like we pass by the mirror
In our homes
And find one,

Yep, even right there in the bathroom
As you rinse,
Looking back at you.

Cups

Easily found all around,
And still

So sacred.

Like temples

Fillings

Medical talks, dentist visits are always hard
Because they often lead to talk about your fillings
That you need to fill
Up to cover up the holes.

But there are holes
To that logic

Like the one new dentist (in a new state) gave to me recently:
I notice when you talk
That your bottom teeth show.
Most people don't do that, so we need to fix that.

(To which) It was unclear if she meant
That they don't talk
Or that they don't show
Their bottom teeth—maybe to hide the fillings.

So to her, I said
Nothing but a smile, closed.

Then she, of course, talked about fillings

That I actually don't need
To fill because I've kept my mouth in check.

And then, naturally
I paid the check,
The bill to fill her pockets
And told them I'll be back in six months
To which the hygienist (her native tongue, Midwestern like me)
Gave me a hug

And left me wondering as I exited
If it was for keeping their mouths fed
Or for keeping my mouth clean
Or for keeping my mouth
Shut.

Maybe I'll ask when I come back in six months
Possibly, for Invisalign
Because the dentist saw when I opened my
Mouth that
I'm crooked, on the bottom teeth.
The only time
They encourage me to open up
My mouth
So that something else
Can be washed away in the cup of fluoride they give—
Maybe even some fragments of it
Into their pockets.

There once was a time

You had a cup.

Then someone–or a few
Came along
And put in their fill and told you
With so much self-satisfaction

'Now,
That cup is mine.'

But what they forgot
And you did, too,
Is that the cup
Is what holds the liquid
And just as so,
It can get rid of it
If the fill doesn't satisfy the one it was poured into.

"Now,

That cup is *mine*."

Once again

Because now you remember,
It always was,

It always has been.

Message in a Bottle: For those of us not much into rain

If I had a grain
Of salt
For every
Particle of rain
Or wave that brushed against my hands

I'd have a cup
Runneth over

And wonder

Why that rain or that wave ever greeted me
With everything I didn't want

And took everything I needed

Instead of passing by

(With the seashells
That was mine.)

Because now, I'm
Left with a vessel of water

But it's water I cannot drink.

Quiet in the library

I went to the library
For the first time
In a long time

And I expected the silence.

The rumination
Over hard, complex things
Or trying to memorize
All that lies
Within, covered.

But what I didn't expect
Were
The books
Still there.

Each one with hard covers
About cups

All cups
That you couldn't see on the outside.
They were only discussed inside.

But you'd have to open each cover,
Every single one of them

And that would be too much
Rumination,
Hardness,
Complexity,
Memories
To relive

In just one visit.
Plus, cups can cause noise

If you open each cover,
Leaving each cup exposed,
one right up next to the other.

I'll have to come back
When the books have been refilled
With less fragile cups,
Maybe plastic instead of ceramic

Or maybe
Some other time.

1 Cup of No-Lyes (Gets in the Eyes)

Is passed around
In the beauty supply
salons
about how we
"Gotta suffer a lil pain for a lil beauty."
Well, that might not be a full lie

But we
also widely decree
We will be gentler with ourselves,
cover ourselves in all things cocoa butter, shea, affirma
tions, intention, and Vitamin E, new conditioning

We won't be
Fooled thrice by **him**, *HER,* triethylamine

We won't worry our pretty little heads
with things our grandmothers, mothers faced,

Won't let any of that mess happen again
not on our watch
certainly not

on our hands

we count all of the mess
dripping off
in goops
onto those heads
Nonetheless, more or less,
engrossing the temples
getting into those eyes

like a baptismal

Well, it used to be,
a lot more than it be
now

But that's less lies
Not no lies

Because some (little white) lye
is still passed around.

Lucky Strike

We gotta knock it all down.
It's no fun, no challenge if we don't.

But I wonder
If we'd still want to play this game
If

What was simply trying to remain
Standing at the end of that long run, stretch

Was our tongues or our canals

That we're so hard-pressed on
Demolishing
Or making
Obliterated piles
For someone else's latest score
to knock down and build something they've been banking on
Or just banking on
Seeing us run dry.

So I'm glad I don't get too many strikes.

For that, I consider myself more than a winner or a player

I consider myself
Lucky.

A Walk in the Park

No one said it would be easy

Learning how to swing,
Push our limbs to the next level
Imagine something greater at the top
After giving it our all

To better feel,
See that brightness
Always waiting to greet us

But instead, we might get rain at first
Reminding us that we have one more sip to drink

Than we estimated, to steady us for the feat.

'Cause shine
Or rain

Young or seasoned
We gotta continue to explore
And test out our bodies to uncover just how great
We are

Until we finally
Don't have to think about it,
Work at it,
Question it

Like muscle memory.

Sometimes I try this

I sometimes carry
A vessel
That's clear

And then try to walk as narrow
And straight
As I can
Or sometimes with a bit of a sway

To see if right then
And there, I'll be asked if I'm alright
Or if I'll be detained.

To see if anyone will think I'm crying out for help
Or crying out for attention
Or just am a crying
Shame.

And so, right then
I produce on cue
Liquid in my eyes
Much more than the liquid
That's left inside
My
Vessel

To see
If they can only see
When now, I myself,
No longer can.

Are you man (OR *WOMAN*) enough?

YOU BETTER FILL OUT THAT CUP
THAT'S RIGHT
FILL IT UP
FILL IT UP
WITH ALL OF THAT JUNK

WITH ALL THAT YOU'RE MADE OF
MORE THAN THAT JOCKSTRAP
OR THAT OTHER KIND OF CUP

FILL IT UP
FILL IT UP
WITH ALL OF THAT JUNK

AND IF YOU
TAKE IT ALL DOWN
YOU'LL GET SOMETHING LIKE
A HIGH-FIVE
SOMETHING LIKE
A HOME RUN FOR GOING TO BAT
GETTING TO HOME
BASE

THAT'S THE WAY

FILL IT UP
FILL IT UP
ALL OF THAT JUNK
FILL IT UP
FILL IT UP
AND THEN TAKE IT ALL DOWN

That there road...

On the other side of town
Something's waiting for you
Something like
A big win
To take home with you
In your trunk

If you make it
After taking it
All the way down

...Good luck.

Filling Station

Had a long ride, huh? Just trying to get back home. I bet.

Yeah,…I bet. Almost gettin' dark around here, sun's bouta set.

Yeah,… sure wish I could get on headed like you.

Ah, not hearin' it. You have so much ahead of you.

Like that road.

But listen, enough of that,

Not what you came in for, right? Came to grab your change

Then get on back

To it. Well, hey

Listen, before you hit the road,

that long road,

help yourself to some of that there premium roast. It's the best brew in town.

Yessir, only the finest fill for your tank. The finest fill around.

'Cause like our slogan says:

"If you're looking for somewhere to fill up

You can always start or stop here."

Alright, well maybe next time.

But remember: We're open 24/7. Always here.

…Safe travels.

Bring It Back Home

Last night, I heard the earth

From inside.
Sometimes, you just have to

Listen more closely.

And there it was:
Rain.

Then when it grows quiet,
Outside
Really quiet
Often at night

If you listen closely,
It's listening, too.

It hears you.

It hears your rain,
Too.

We just call ours

Pain.

The Stories We Grew Up On...

To be

Tipped over
Poured out

Even as kids,
We're already doing it:
Have to worry about our cups.

Maybe
It's time
To change that.

Maybe

With a shout.

Here's How I Make My Tea

First,

I'll have you know I don't like just any old kind.

Those who know
Me
Know
That there's a very particular relationship
Between
Tea
And
I
Only welcome the

Following
Ingredients:

Into my cup,

A little lemon (for immunity)
Agave (to still experience some good)
Not hot and cold
Just one goes
For me

Fill me
Up

Filling my cup
With tea

But not with just any old thing
Particular about what I allow into my cup

And hoping you do the same.

That's why I shared my recipe.

KEELA BUFORD

Heeled

I searched for it today

That one ~~thing~~

That same one

I always do

That one

that always stays

But today

I could no longer find it,

That one

thing on my heel

Think it finally washed away

with the Epsom salt

or the fluoride

or the stale tea

How is your cup looking
now? Share with us.

KEELA BUFORD
is the author of *Pride, and Joy*
(yes, the comma is intentional),
somewhat like the historical sister novel to her
second novel, *The Buy-In*. She is a content specialist
who has helped many businesses in vast
industries. Her creative and screenplay works have
placed in semifinalist positions with Stage 32,
WeScreenplay, Outfest, and IndieFEST.